Two Hours To Live

Two Hours • One Demand • No Second Chances

First Edition

Created by Joseph N Burton

Chapter 1

I stride down the jetty, bag in hand.
My shoes scrape against the weathered wood. Sunlight
tickles the back of my neck.
The taste of salt on my tongue and the hush of ocean waves
on the white sand shore soothe me. The edge of the dock
beckons, along with the sanctity of silence.

Man, this vacation has been a long time coming. With the
divorce and Amy's outrageous settlement, not to mention the
media coverage, I deserve a damn break.
Never mind. It's taken the last of my savings to get me to my
small corner of paradise - a remote island off the coast of
Cuba.

No one will find me here.

I can finally take a second to gather my thoughts. "A time
out before the next movie," I mutter as I run my fingers
through my salt-slicked hair.

As the ocean breeze pushes me onward, I step off the jetty
and onto the pitted 'crete of the dock.
The place is basically empty, apart from a couple stragglers.
"Strange," I whisper.

"Excuse me," a man says at the end of the walkway. His
white coat sticks out against the backdrop of palms and the
holiday resort against a hill. A couple more feet and it'd be
a mountain.

"Excuse me, are you Jay O'Connor?
I - could I trouble you for an autograph?" the stranger asks
in a British accent.

"Not today," I say and shove away the guilt. My publicist would freak out if she heard me dare refuse an autograph at a time like this.
"Please, I just - I'm such a huge fan." The man steps closer and holds out a pen. The edge of his coat flaps in the breeze.

"Dude, you don't even have a piece of paper. You want me to sign your ass or something? Because I don't play that."
The man grasps my arm. An iron grip too strong for his skinny arms.

"Please," he whispers and brings the pen up.
"What are you doing? Let go of me," I say and glance back at the boat.
It's a speck on the horizon. Panic streaks through my core. I've dealt with crazy fans before, but this takes it to another level.
His brown eyes are wide, filled with desperation, and a hint of something else.

"Just one autograph," the man hisses. Silver glints in my peripheral vision. The nib is too long. The pen – it's too fat.
"That's not a pen," I say stupidly, as he drives the needle into the skin of my neck.

I feel stinging like liquid fire spreading through my veins.
I shudder a gasp and smack his hand, but he doesn't let go.
The man brings his face closer, beads of sweat trickle from his temples beside graying hair.

"Listen carefully," he says, in a throat-scratching tone.
"I've injected you with a deadly virus.
You have two hours to live.
If you want the cure, you must pay me five million dollars."
"Wait. Wha -?"
The man's grip tightens.

Two Hours to Live

Wind brushes the back of my neck.
Pressure builds between us.
"Two hours. Pay up or you'll die."

"Bastard," I grunt. This is my life.
Always some guy looking for a handout.
He's probably injected me with sugar water or some shit.

It's a scam.

I've been through this type of thing before.
Not the needle, but the blackmail.
"What is this?"

The scientist slides the needle from my skin.
He pockets the syringe and pats it once.
"Five million dollars," he says.
"Come with me, and I'll give you the payment details.
I'll create the cure."

"Cure? For what?
What is this? What did you put inside me?"
I press my palm to my neck.
Wetness trickles between my fingers. I pull my hand back,
but it's clean and dry.

"There will be side effects."

The scientist steps closer again, and I flinch. "Don't make
this complicated. You'll die if we don't hurry."

It's the third time he's said that.
It finally hits home.

I raise my fist and cut upward toward his square chin. He
dodges back, out of reach.

Two Hours to Live

My knuckles connect with thin air and I spin on the spot and stumble, falling to my knees on the dock.

The concrete scrapes my chinos, the tear of fabric and grind of flesh jar my senses.
I teeter forward and flop onto my stomach. So much for the new Ralph Lauren shirt.
My bag falls from my hand and bounces out of reach.

"Don't exert yourself too much," the scientist says.

I focus on the pair of jeans which poke from the bottom of his lab coat.
They haze out of view then back again.

"What the hell is this?"
And this time, my concern is as real as the blood in my veins.
 "It's a virus," the scientist says. He drops to his haunches in front of me.

A flash of pity mars that façade of severity.

"It will eat you from the inside out. Your side effects will worsen the closer you get to the two-hour deadline."

I scuffle to my hands and knees and dive at him again. He's not quick enough this time.

We connect, and the scientist flies backward and tumbles along the walkway.
A shocked scream rings out. I raise my head, and a woman swims in and out of my gaze. She stares at us, jaw dropped, then turns to run.
 "Wait." I raise a hand. She can help stop this madness. A witness.
The scientist pushes me back and I land hard on my ass.

"It's no use fighting," he says. "You'll be too weak soon. Come with me. Pay the money. I'll fix you up."
"Why would I trust you?"
I ask between labored breaths.

It's too hot to breathe. No, it's too cold. Ice runs down my spine. More wetness that isn't there.

"Because I'm your only hope." He holds out his clean palm. I stare at it, caught between life and the truth. I don't have the money to pay him.

"Come with me," the scientist says and jerks his hand closer.

I reach for it.

Chapter 2

An inhalation and then… an explosion rocks the building in the distance. The swell of sound deafens me and breaks over our bodies.

Orange flames overwhelm the resort, bubbling through the air. Tile shatters, rubble flips end over end. Smoke rises in a pyre.

Distant shrieks are drowned out by the rumble of collapse. I grab for the scientist's hand. He retracts it.

My palms slap against the concrete and I tumble onto my forearms.
"What?" That's all I can say. I stare up at the man who's trying to kill me.

The scientist is as pale as a sheet. "No," he says, and I can barely make out the word.

" Lily!" the man shrieks.
He spins on his heel and darts off toward the burning wreckage, past an elderly couple clinging to each other.

The dock is crowded. People stare, slack-jawed, at the burning wreckage beyond the palms and exotic trees. Slowly, the devastation strikes home.
Eyes widen. Women tremble. Men grasp their partners by the hand. Screams ring out in the vacuum of sound.

"Escorpiones Negros," a man says behind me.

I don't have the energy to turn. I don't care what he means. Instead, I reach for the watch on my left wrist. I twist the dial and set the alarm. "Two hours," I whisper.

My head swims, but the vision clears at last. That side effect has finally faded.

Sirens ring in the distance and hope spears my heart.
It fades again.
They won't be able to help me, if the scientist has to make the cure.

I'm on my own.

"Jill," I say, scrambling across the dock. I push myself upright and limp to my bag.
It's popped open on one side, trampled by a rush of feet. My tablet lies face down beside a rumple of clothes.

"Shit." I turn it over. The screen is cracked. "Shit."
"Are you okay?" An elderly woman bends down beside me and touches my arm.

I snatch it out of reach and glare at her. "Fine," I reply before swallowing. My throat is as scratchy as the desert.

"Let me help you. Do you need an ambulance?" Her accent is thick. English isn't her native language.

I ignore her and rifle through my pockets. I whip out my cellphone and swear again.
The screen isn't just cracked on the cell. It's shattered.
Liquid blues and yellows spread behind the ruined glass, but it still lights up.

That's fine. I know Jill's number by heart.

"Young man, you look like you need to go to the hospital," the woman says.

She hasn't recognized me, by some miracle.

Maybe all that smoke in the distance has wiped the slate clean.
No one cares if you starred in a movie or produced one, when the hotel is on fire.
The woman grasps my arm and I wrench it free. "Get away from me," I hiss.
She stumbles back and presses her palm to her chest.
Confusion radiates from her.
She doesn't have anything on me.

"Focus," I whisper, blocking out the sirens and screams. The scent of thick smoke drifts on the sea breeze.
Burnt salt, this time. "Jill."

I type in her number on the keypad. I press the phone icon and raise the cell to my ear.
Nothing happens. No ringing. No annoying nasal whine from my assistant.

"Shit." I drop the phone from my face. I slip it back into my pocket, who the hell knows why, and stare up at the resort.
Is there even a cell signal in this God forsaken place?

I've got to find him. Money or no money, I have to find the scientist guy or I'm going to die.

"Why is this happening, Mommy?" A little boy wails nearby and grips his mother's hand.
She touches his white, blond hair and squeezes her eyes shut.
No one has the answer.

I stumble along the dock and leave the ruins of my bag behind. I check my watch and swallow.

Six minutes have passed since that bastard speared me in the neck.
Snatches of information drift past me. My mind grasps the tail ends of conversations.
"… drug cartel."
"But why would they blow up the hotel?"

I swim past the noises and quicken my pace. My breaths come fast but ragged. My heart skips two beats.
I quash the panic. Focus. I'll find him and get the cure.

Disjointed thoughts.

Why would he do this? Does he need the money for something or –?
"A war," a man says to my right.
People raise their palms to shield their eyes from the sun.

"When will the boats come?" another person asks.
"An hour," the reply comes, deadpan. People are numb. The shrieks have ended.
They stare at the burning wreckage ahead and inch further back, distancing themselves from the horror.

I push on in the opposite direction, toward the cloud of destruction and the burning tops of trees in the jungle which engulf the island.

A hand grips my ruined Ralph Lauren shirt. "You can't go that way," he says. "You'll die. It's too dangerous."

I shake him off and resist the urge to check my watch again.
"Almost there," I whisper the empty encouragement.
Amy would laugh if she could see me now. "The glorious Jay O' Connor," she would say,

in a mocking tone, every chance she got. "What's the matter, Jay? Things not going your way?"

"Leave me alone," I whisper.

But her voice doesn't fade. The words ring through my consciousness and curl around the base of my spine, taunting me. "Jay O'Connor, afraid? I don't believe it."

This has got to be a side effect of the disease. I'm losing my mind.

"Jay O'Connor doesn't have a plan?" My ex-wife's laughter rings through my head. "Poor baby."

I speed up to a jog and disappear between the trees.

Chapter 3

Leaves brush against my shirt. Moisture drifts between the trunks and across the damp ground.
It's too humid to function.

I unbutton my shirt and roll up my sleeves, but my fingers fumble on the cuffs.

Smoke is thick on the air. I'm closer now. The screams are clearer; the sirens too. How many people have died?

What if the scientist is one of them?
My heart palpitates, and I check the watch on my wrist – Tag Heuer, of course – and gulp. Another six minutes have passed.

Birds whoop and call in the canopy, unconcerned by the mayhem nearby.
Or by my impending death.

I quicken my pace and burst through the line of trees, out into the open.

The wreckage of the hotel screams into my consciousness. There are bodies on the floor in front of it.

Blood stained, peppered with debris. People are dying in front of me and there's nothing I can do to help.

I don't have time for this.

An ambulance parks in front of the ruined hotel. The flashing lights of a fire truck
glance off the windows, and I squint and avert my eyes.
"Where the hell are you?" I whisper.

I jog toward the side of the building and stop short of the wreckage. One side of the hotel is still intact.
The other burns and crumbles. It's a scene from one of my apocalyptic movies. The one that tanked at the box office.

On the left, the world burns, palm trees on fire, steel melting. On the right, people stumble out of the hotel, coughing, chased by dry heat from the fire.

"Where?" I can't form a full sentence. I have to find him. He ran this way. He has to be here.

I peer through the open door and into the lobby. Lights swing from the ceiling, and the polished reception desk is empty.
A wood-backed sofa lingers beside a coffee table.
Everyone is gone.
No glimpse of a white coat.
Silence thunders in my ears. The sirens outside are gone, and the rush of burning is muted here.
The scent of smoke, fainting.

"Hello?" I step over the threshold. I don't even know the guy's name to call him.
"Uh – scientist?"
My watch beeps. Time is running out. I check it and twist the dial again.
An alarm for every ten minutes. I have to know how close I am.
No time to fool around. It's pretty much black and white right now.
There is no gray area. Find the cure or die.

Sweat trickles down my spine. Another cold flush travels over my skin.
"Is anyone in here?" I cup my hands at both sides of my mouth and project my voice through the empty lobby.

Two Hours to Live

 Bloodied fingers grasp my arm and dig into my flesh.
The world freezes. My eyes bulge outward.

"What the hell." I shriek and tug free. Adrenaline soars
through my bloodstream.
Images of the needle float in front of my eyes.

The tiled floor tips up to greet me.

"Help," a voice says. The grip lands on my forearm again
and blood smears my skin.
"Please, you have to help."

I sway on the spot, teetering on the brink of vertigo and
nausea.

A woman stands beside me, bleeding from a gash on her
forehead. The flow drips instead of flows, marring her right
eye.
She blinks the blood and stares at me. She sways on the spot
too.

Her dark hair hangs loose around her shoulders, coated in a
fine layer of white dust.
She must've come from the other side of the resort. The
apocalyptic side.

"What do you want?" I tug at her grip again, but my fingers
are so damn weak.

"Help. You have to help," she says. Her voice fades in and
out.

"There's an ambulance outside.
Let go of me," I reply.

She doesn't.

"It's gone. Ambulance is gone. Fire truck is gone. No one else here to save us now.
So many people are dying.
Please, you have to help us."
She drops to her knees and finally releases my arm.
She grabs at her stomach instead and drags at her cotton shirt, printed with the hotel's palm tree logo.

Blood stains it. She parts the tattered edges. The mass of flesh beneath is barely visible.
A gash covered in blood. The edge of something sharp juts out of her.
I gag and look away.
"I can't go on," she says. "Please, help."

There's nothing I can do to help her. She's going to die, with or without an ambulance.

"There's a radio," she says.

I focus on her again – and thank God – she's dropped the tattered edges of her shirt. The wound is covered.

"What?"

"Call the mainland," she says and raises a finger.
"Communication room. Radio that way."
Her breaths rattle in and out of her mouth.
She winces and grabs her stomach. "More hurt."

A radio.

The woman keels over onto her side. I take a step toward her, but she shakes her head.

"Go. Quick. Before they come."
"Who?" I ask.
She shakes her head again.
"Who's coming?"

"Escorpiones Negros," she hisses, and the air leaks from her lungs. She shuts her eyes and goes somewhere else.
It's a place I can't reach her. Her face relaxes into a semblance of peace.
The blood puddles beneath her body.
It's the second time someone has said 'Escorpiones Negros' in the last fifteen minutes.
I don't want to find out what it means. I don't want to be around long enough to find out.
I turn, and my shoes squeak on the lobby tiles. Spotless in the wake of destruction, apart from the splatters of blood.

The radio. Maybe I can call the mainland, tell them about the injection. Get help. Get hold of Jill to get me money.

The thoughts sink into my stomach and settle like lead. There's no hope left. I check my watch and swallow.
Minutes tick by.

Got to be faster than this. Have to find him before it's too late.

Chapter 4

The radio room is in an office behind the reception desk. The window looks out on the encroaching jungle.

Smoke drifts past and blocks my view of a swatch of palm trees. I cough and ignore the pounding of my heart.
A skipped beat, several in quick succession, another skipped beat.

I grab the microphone, and the twisted cord springs in response.
I press the button on the side of the receiver, but nothing happens.

"It's not on," I say to myself. I can't make sense of anything right now. That scientist has dulled my senses.

I bend toward the radio and fiddle with the switch. Orange light flares behind the front panel and digits flash on the screen.
At last, it's on now. I don't twiddle the dials.
Chances are that the radio has been kept on this frequency for a reason. Contact with the mainland.

I ignore the book of codes beside the compact, black device, and instead, click the button on the side of the radio.

"Hello, can anyone hear me?" I say. Genius introduction. Man, no wonder I star in hit movies on the big screen.
I have the best words. "This is Jay O'Connor." Not that it matters.

Radio static crackles through the speaker.

"Hello, I'm here at the Hotel Flamenco on Cayo Largo.

We need help. There's been an explosion.
People are dying.
Please, we need help." What else can I say? "I've been
stabbed, uh, injected with poison. No, a disease."

God, this sounds ridiculous. I release the button and lean my
fists on the squat, wooden table.

The radio crackles, and a voice comes over the waves, deep
and broken by bad reception.
"This is the Cuban Coast Guard," the man says. "Please
describe your issue again, over."

Miracles do exist.

I raise the receiver again and click the button. "I'm on Cayo
Largo.
There's been an explosion here at the hotel. I – we need help.
Send an ambulance, and uh, I –"
I cut off because how the hell am I supposed to segue into
my problem?

"We're aware of this issue," the man replies. "Help is on the
way for those who have survived the attack. Over."

"Attack? What do you mean an attack?" My stomach turns,
and bile rises in the back of my throat. "Who's attacked?"

"Sir, please remain calm," the man replies. His tone sobers.
"Is there anything else you need help with? Over."

I raise my left arm and gaze at the minute hand of my watch.
The alarm hasn't yet gone off again.

I click the button, and the plastic jams against my thumb.
"I – someone injected me with something bad.

I need help too. I need to speak to someone who can contact my assistant." That's the best way to put it.
Anything else sounds crazy.

More static crackles, and my insides turn to jelly. I need a reply on this. "Hello?" My finger trembles against the plastic button.
I gaze out of the window.
"Can you hear me? Uh – over."

"We hear you," the voice says. "We hear you and we're coming for you."

It doesn't bring me relief. The guy on the end of the line hasn't said 'over' this time. I open my mouth and shut it again.

"Pay the money, Mr. O'Connor," the voice says. "Pay the money and you'll be fine."

"Who is this?" Heat runs through me this time. A warning flash of adrenaline. What the hell is going on? "Why are you doing this?"

"Money. Pay it and you live. We're on our way to you now." The accent is thickened by laughter.

Panic closes in on me and strangles my thoughts. "This isn't a game. We need help here. People are dying."

"And you're next."

I drop the receiver, and the plastic clatters on the desk. I jam my finger against the switch.
The orange light behind the panel disappears. Tires screech somewhere nearby. Gravel crunches under boots.

It can't be them. Whoever 'they' are.

I back toward the door of the office and peer out into the lobby. A jeep stands outside the shattered front doors.
Fumes pour out its tail pipe. Two men dressed in camo pants and black tanks pile out of the vehicle.
 They lift automatic rifles. I can't make out what type of rifles they are from here. I don't want to.

I dart back, out of sight.
The men speak to each other in Spanish. Their voices grow louder. The front door slams open and glass crunches beneath heavy boots.

"- close." They switch to English.

"Gringo… kill him if he makes the wrong move."

I stumble back and bump into the desk. A cup tips onto its side and rolls toward the edge of the table.
It drops off the edge. I catch it before it strikes the ground. I freeze.
The footsteps crunch closer.

I glance over my shoulder toward the window. A flash of white between the trees. A man retreating into the jungle.
The scientist?

I put down the mug and dart for the windows. I crash them open, slip out, and drop to the paving stones below.
"Wait," I whisper. I've got to stop him before he disappears again. Why would he tell me to pay up then run away?

He screamed the name 'Lily'. Who is she? She must have something to do with the disease.

The men enter the office, and their steps echo above my head. If I move, they'll see me. If I stay, the scientist will disappear, and my last hope will be gone.

My watch alarm screeches a ten-minute warning.

"Outside," one of the armed men shouts.
I scramble upright and launch myself toward the tree line.

Shots pop at both sides of me, and a bullet zips past my ear and punctures the trunk of a tree. I zig-zag, left and right; gotta throw them off.
The trees are so close. Pain spears my mind, but it's not a shot. It's the disease.

Gunfire follows me, the bullets spit dirt in my wake.

I dive into the forest.

Chapter 5

"You think you're better than everyone else, Jay."
Amy's voice chases me through the trees, and by the dappled light which filters between the canopy leaves.

Nausea takes hold of my stomach, growing stronger by the second. "You think you're more important."

"Stop," I mutter.

The gunfire has halted.
I grab hold of a tree trunk and dig my fingers into the rough bark.
Leaves, muck, and dried, broken vines litter the path ahead, but it gives me hope.

There's a path. There wouldn't be a path unless someone uses it.
I raise my watch and the face blurs. I blink as my vision clears after a second.

"One hour, thirty minutes to live."

"You call that living?" Amy asks, in my mind. "You call anything that's happened in your life, living? Pathetic."
"Piss off, Amy." I stumble up the path.
Footsteps thump ahead of me and I freeze. Is this a side effect of the disease?
I'm going mad.

Amy's already in my brain, and now, she's probably materialized outside of it.
God, that's the last company I want right now.

Two Hours to Live

I hurry up the path, which curls through the forest and along
the side of the hill.
Wood from the ground every few feet – are these steps?
The trees are close here, but I catch a flicker of movement
out of the corner of my eye.
"Hello?!" I yell.

"Yeah, that's a good idea," Amy whispers in my ear.
"Scream real loud. They won't find you then."
I wave a hand beside my ear, but she isn't there. Of course,
she isn't there.
She's back in L.A. doing what she does best. Gym instruc-
tors.

A fly buzzes nearby and lands on my cheek. I swat it but
miss.
Footsteps again, further up the path.
I jog after them, pulse skipping again. Nausea bubbles in my
stomach and acid travels up my throat and collects in the
back of my mouth.

I turn and vomit on the ground, then wipe my mouth with
the back of my hand.

"Oh, how the mighty have fallen," Amy hisses. "You always
thought you were better than me, Jay."
"You said that already," I whisper back. Crazy to talk to
myself. It must be a side effect. That's all.

Nausea, palpitating heart, sweat, cold flushes, and insanity.
Just another walk in the park.

"Oh did I?" Amy asks, in her usual nasal whine.
What did I ever see in the woman?
"You need plenty of reminders," she says.

"Too busy for me. You're always too busy for everyone. Good thing we didn't get pregnant."

"God forbid."

I run up the path and pump my arms back and forth. Weakness drags me back and I swallow reflexively. The nasty taste in my mouth doesn't fade.
"They're going to catch you, you know," Amy whispers. Wind brushes the back of my neck.

It's like she's here with me, for real. I want to rip my ears off.

I reach a plateau and carry on down the path at a jog. My legs wobble and I misstep, but I don't stop. No time for that.

A house appears between the trees. No, it's not a house. A bunker.
It's shrouded by the low-hanging branches and made of gray concrete.
The metal roof is flat and dull in the lack of sunlight.

A single window peers out of the side, frameless, and a metal door stands ajar beside it.

"Sure, that looks safe," Amy says. "You go on in and make some friends.
You'll have a great time."

"You're such a bitch."

I shuffle across the grass. I can't afford to move carefully, but I slow my steps anyway.

Another path stretches from the corner of the house, wider than the one I followed here. It's big enough for a car, but there isn't one parked nearby.

Bird calls pierce the silence, along with the rustle of little paws in the undergrowth.
Please let it be paws and nothing else.

I creep toward the front door. No use knocking. I push it open, and it squeals on rusted hinges.
The noise sets my teeth against each other. I glance over my shoulder, but empty forest greets me.

Branches, leaves, mud, and the edge of the path. The armed men haven't followed, yet.
"They'll come," Amy hisses. "And then you'll die.
You deserve every bit of pain.
You ruined everything between us. You ruined everything with your family."

Tears sting the corners of my eyes. I force my mind to focus.

I step into the bunker and halt. Gloomy inhabits a single room. It stretched from the corners to the ceiling and coursed across that too.

I walk to the desk in the corner. A computer sits on top of it, but the power button doesn't work.
Next to it, a framed picture springs into view. I grab it and stare at the people in the image.

Three of them. One is the scientist, the other a beautiful woman with long, dark hair, and the other a girl.
The scientist's hand rests on the girl's shoulder, and a huge smile stretches across his face. No lab coat.

They're not on an island in the picture, either. They're in front of a brick house, with a white picket fence. An oak tree loses its leaves in the corner of the picture, a swing attached to one of its branches.
Home.

"What is this place?" I put the picture frame back where it came from and spin on the spot. My hands tremble.
Boxes are piled beneath the empty window. A rumpled bunk bed is squished into the corner.

The man has a family. The man has a livelihood. How in God's name did he end up here?
"Sympathy? From you? Impossible. You're only after the cure, remember? You don't care about the man's family," Amy says.

Her voice echoes outside of my mind this time and I glance over my shoulder. My gaze rests on the picture again.
I disconnect from the moment and the man in the image and walk to the boxes instead.
I grasp the top one and rip back the cardboard.
Packing material pops out. I rip it free and litter it to the floor.

Books are stacked inside. Journals, each labeled with a year. I grab the one on top and flip it open. My gaze tracks across the page.

It's our last day at home. "It must be the doctor writing." I don't want to leave but I don't have a choice.
Eliana's brother has brought this hell upon us. If we don't follow through, he'll die.

She'll never forgive me. I must do what's best for my family, but if I go, we'll all regret it.

I snap the journal shut and put it on top of the pile. My head pounds and I reach up, grab it between my fingers and squeeze.
I don't need this pressure. I don't want to feel this way about the scientist.

My watch beeps once.

Car doors slam outside.

"They're here," Amy whisper, and giggles with delight. "They've come for you, you bastard."

Chapter 6

I drop to all fours and exhale through my mouth. I can't trust anyone here.
Not the scientist, not the thugs with the guns, not the so-called Coast Guard.
Chances are, whoever's outside the bunker doesn't want to be my best friend.

I crawl to the space beneath the window, then rise slowly, until the top of my head peeks above the grey sill.

A car hums outside. The same one that was parked outside the hotel. Or one exactly like it.
The two men in camo and black shirts are identical. They could be part of something bigger, but it doesn't matter.
The only thing that registers is 'guns'.

I crouch down again and sneak toward the doorway. My palms slip on the cement and scrape across dirt.
I freeze and strain my ears for movement.

Dull chatter drifts through the door, becoming sharper the closer I get.
The accents are the same heavy ones which came through the radio.

They're in control here, whoever the hell they are.

I halt just beside it, get into a crouch, and tense every muscle in my body.
"Boss says if the deal go south, we gotta do it," a thug says.
I can't see which one, and frankly, I don't care.
Every part of me aches to run, but I can't. Hopefully, they'll leave.
"Where is he?" another voice utters.

From thug number two. "The place looks deserted."
"He is looking for his girl now.
That Eliana bitch is dead, so the girl is all he has for now."

Thug number one snickers and re-adjusts his grip on the rifle. It clicks against his side.

The name 'Eliana' rings through my mind. It isn't the one the scientist screamed after the explosion, but it belongs to a woman.
The wife? The daughter?
Is his family in danger? It doesn't matter.
"Of course, it doesn't," Amy whispers. "You don't care about anyone but yourself."

I check my watch. It'll go off soon, and I don't need to be discovered right now. I punch the button to stop it before it can go off.

"We kill the other one too?" thug number two asks.
I focus on their conversation again, but my skin crawls – part a desperate need to be away from this place and part side effect.
Pinpricks run down my body. Agony follows, and I jam my lips together to keep from crying out.

"Like I said, if the deal falls through, she dies. That's all that matter to the boss," thug one says.
"It's a girl."
"You goin' soft, hombre?" Thug one's tone hops with mirth. He clacks his weapon again. "Ain't no room for pussies aroun' here."

"Look, man," thug two replies, "I jus' don't like to kill the little ones. I got a cousin, man."

"Okay, you explain to the boss how you can't do the job 'cos of your baby cousin." Thug one can't contain his laughter.

"I kill you next, you lil' bitch," thug two replies.

They both break into a raucous bout of laughter which trickles through the open door and dances toward me.

"C'mon, we check out the place. If he is not in there, maybe we will find the girl."

The girl from the photo? I glance around the small interior, but it's empty, except for the morbid furniture.
There's no girl here. There's only me, and I'm about to get shot up or captured.

"Hol' on. I wanna light my smoke," thug two says. "I left the lighter in the car."
"Hurry up," thug one responds and clicks his tongue.

Pressure builds behind my eyes. They're coming in.
I poke my head around the corner. Their backs are turned.

Thug two heads toward the parked jeep. Thug one examines the side of his sleek, black rifle.
He whistles under his breath, and the noise floats on a cloud of humidity.

Now's my chance.

"You're going to die," Amy whispers.

I burst into motion and sprint out the door, past the man with the gun.
He spins toward me and squeezes the trigger. Bullets pop in rapid succession.

Thug one yells something inaudible.

I scrape against a tree and collapse. My back hits the ground first.
I roll onto my front and the momentum carries me down the hill.
Trees flip past; the world is upside down then right side up.

I open my eyes and try to grab onto something, but it doesn't work.
My fingers rip against a sharp rock.
I flail.
A tree swings toward me.
My head bangs into it.

"Told you," Amy hisses. "You're dead now."

Blackness.

Chapter 7

I float on waves in the darkness. They lap at me and tug at my arms. Muffled voices and the crunch of boots on twigs and dirt reverberate through my mind.
"There you are," Amy says.

The gloom is gone, and I'm in our living room again. Amy's sprawled across the white sofa, her dainty toes – fairies, as I always call them – twiddling in time to the beat of the music from the stereo I insisted on keeping, even though we can afford a new one. Or can we?

A thrill ripples through the room and the edges blur.

"What are you doing here?" I ask. And why do I remember this day?
"What are you talking about, hon?" Amy asks. Her laugh tinkles through the space, past the crystal-topped coffee table. "I live here. Hello? Did you bump your head shooting today?"

I stare at her blankly. Anger swells in my stomach. I take the brown folder out from underneath my arm and brandish it.
"What's that?" Amy asks. Fear tinges her tone for the first time. She sits up straight and braces the heels of her palms on the sofa.

"I know about him," I say, and the memories rush into existence. "I hired an investigator, Amy."
"W-wha –" She cuts off and clenches her jaw. "I don't know what you're talking about."
 "You're sleeping with him. Your instructor. I've got pictures. Photographic evidence, Amy."

She glares at me and opens her mouth. She shuts it again and chews on her words. What can she possibly say to me about this?

 "You thought I wouldn't find out about this?"
I scoff, but the humor is a façade. I love this woman. No, I loved her. I gave her everything, and this is how she repays me.
"You wanted this to happen," she replies, forcing herself upright.
I actually take a step back. "What?"
"You pushed me away.
Ever since your mother –"
"Don't bring her into this."

"Ever since that old battle axe died, you've treated me like an outsider. She hated me, didn't she?" Amy folds her arm beneath her breasts.
I lower my head and sigh. "Yeah. She hated you. She warned me you'd do something like this. I should've listened."

"Don't start this remorseful trip now. You weren't there for her when she was on the way out. You ignored her. You can't pretend you care now," Amy says and rolls her eyes at me.
How does she always manage to do this? She turns everything around on me.
"You know what this means, right?" I ask.
Amy glances down at the ring finger on her left hand. A slow smile creeps across her face. She meets my gaze again. "I get half of everything."

Blackness again.

A jarring sensation of wrongness. The scent of wet mulch and earthy mud. Grit between my teeth.

I open my eyes and stare at the dark green fronds above my head. They brush my face, and light pierces the spaces between their fingers.

I'm not in my mini mansion in L.A. I'm on a remote Cuban island, hunted by killers, hours from death.

"Shit," I whisper. How long was I out?

Pain throbs in the back of my head. I lift my left arm and hover the watch in front of my eyes.

I've been out for five minutes. Time is running out. Less than an hour and a half until the side effects fade, and I'm embraced by that blackness for good this time.

I work my jaw, reach up, and touch the stubble on my chin.

I'm tucked in between two roots at the base of a tree.

I twiddle my toes and they move, thank God. I bend both knees and tuck them toward my chest.

Footsteps scrape along the ground nearby, behind my hiding spot.

"He gotta be nearby," a man says. Sounds like thug number two. Same dulcet tones.

"We find him. We take him to the warehouse and get our money. Maybe we get a little extra," thug one says.

"How we get the money if we don' have the scientist?" Thug two halts behind my tree. His breaths are loud and labored.

They make my stomach turn. They'll find me. There's no way I'm getting out of this one.

Thug number one replies in Spanish, but it's all a mess in my mind. I don't have any knowledge of the language.

What little I learned in school has flown out of my ear and into the afternoon.

Sweat puddles between my ass cheeks. I struggle against the itch to run.

"Vámonos," thug one says. He jams the butt of his rifle against my tree.

The men walk further down, away from my position. I don't dare breathe. I refuse relief in case they sense it somehow.
Their heavy steps fade, bit by bit, and the noise is replaced by the whoop of the birds in the trees. A howl of some other animal pierces the air. I flinch.
These sounds would be comforting at another time.

I inhale once, twice through my nose, then sit up slowly. The trees are silent watchers, judging my next move.

My watch alarm beeps, and I shut it off.
"Where are you?" I whisper.
The scientist's bunker is nearby but empty. I probably could turn myself over to those thugs, but I've got the feeling they're going to want more than I can give them.
That scientist… he isn't too big. He doesn't have a weapon.

Maybe, just maybe, I can force him to give me the cure, without paying up.

"First I have to find him." I grasp two handfuls of grass and use them as leverage. I manage to stand. My head pounds but I ignore it.
Voices drift toward me. The thugs are on their way back.

I hurry between the trunks and undergrowth, away from the noises and into the murk.

I have to keep moving.

Chapter 8

The forest blurs past me. Splashes of brown and green, the occasional jarring yellow or red from a bird or a fruit of some kind. I'm moving now. I'm not moving, I'm flying. My thoughts race.
I'm on fire. My skin prickles and I pat my arms. No fire, just another side effect.

Adrenaline squirms through my veins, forcing one foot in front of the other. The ache in my head is gone. Or it's there, and I just can't feel it. I'm on another high.
It's got to be a part of the disease. God knows what will happen when it stops, and I crash back down to Earth.

I rush past another tree and bump my arm. A quick flare of pain. It vanishes again and I jog onward. Down the hill, toward that breeze.

The smell of the ocean draws me to it. It has a feeling of 'rightness' about it.

I dodge past a low-lying branch and hop over a rock ensconced in mud. My phone buzzes in the front right pocket of my stained pants.

"What?" I halt, and it's like two trains colliding. Every bone in my body tries to move forward, downhill, to that salty smell, but my skin and flesh stays in place.
"What is that?"

My phone!

I grasp the rectangular shape and worm it out of my pocket.

The screen flashes, though the blue, green, and yellow colors which leak across the screen don't make any sense. It's still cracked.

How is it even working right now?
My fingers tremble. I press the icon and raise the phone to my ear.
"Hello?" My voice croaks more than I'd like. I clear it. "Hello?" My muscles tense up – I can't be too loud. The thugs might hear me and come running. Who knows how many of them there are.

The reception crackles and cuts out, then crackles again.
Shit. Are there any cell towers on this damn island? I don't remember anything about Wi-Fi or connectivity at the resort.

"Hello? This is Jay O'Connor." I gulp down wet air, the kind that sticks to the insides of my esophagus and clogs my mouth.
"Jay?" Oh man, Holy God.
It's Jill, my secretary.
"Jill!" I clap my hand to my mouth to block out further outbursts. "Jill, listen, I'm in a lot of trouble. Someone's poisoned me, I don't know. I need money. A lot of it."

The line crackles again.
I squirm on the spot. Hop from one foot to the other. "Jill, are you there?"

"Jay – everyone's worried – all right?"
"I can barely hear you," I say. "Can you hear me?"
"Where are you?"

She comes through, clearer than before.
"I'm not at the hotel.
Someone blew it up."

"I know." Her reply crackles a little, but at least it's her. It's Jill. —"drug war."

A drug war?

That would imply there's more than one gang running around on the island.

Trust me to get involved in this shit. As if I need more drama in my life.

I check my watch and shift my weight again. "I need money, Jill.

I need you to contact The Brad. Tell him he has to come up with five million dollars.

It's urgent. I don't care if he has to steal it."

The line crackles and my heart sinks. Did she hear a word I said?

"Jill! I need money." Leaves rustle behind me and I duck down. The sudden change in position rocks through my core and I fall onto my knees. "Jill?" I scan the trees, but there's no one in sight.

"- I don't know what you're – look, just call from – I'll speak to –"

Frustration bubbles behind my lips and presses outward. I can't scream at her. This is a waste of time. "Jill. I – need – money," I say, as clearly as I can.

"What?" she yells.

"Money!" I reply, as loudly as I can. That will draw attention. "I'm in trouble. Men are trying to kill me. If I don't pay, I will die."

"How much?"

A sliver of relief through the black despair. She's finally heard me. "Five million dollars."

Two Hours to Live

The line cuts off.

I have no idea if she'll get hold of The Brad. Probably not.
She doesn't know why I need the cash or how to get it to me.

The bird noises now mock me.
Carefree animals. Disease-free.

My stomach clenches, and an ulcerous ache burns down
below. Has the organ eating started? Am I combusting from
the inside out?

I drop the phone to my lap and stare at the cracked screen.
The light behind it is gone. It's just a piece of trash now.
I rise and slip it back into my pocket, more out of habit than
out of use. Maybe it will come in handy.

My headache screams back into existence. The adrenaline
has seeped out and the crash is here.

I grab the tree trunk nearest to me and pull myself toward it.
I slam into its rough bark and press my nose against the
furrows. They remind me of my mother's frown.
The disapproving glare from my adulthood.
Although, it goes back further than that.

Inhale, exhale, not much time left. My mind focuses on the
watch. The alarm will go off soon, won't it?

The forest is my prison now. It slows my progress.
I walk instead of run, force myself to go faster, then slow
again because my muscles are messy bits of nothingness.
They slip around inside my sausage legs and fail me.

I fall to the dirt and get a nose full of the stuff. I lie there for
a second, and the weight of despair crushes me into the earth.

"The fabulous Jay O'Connor," Amy whispers. "Reduced to nothing. You're dirt. Trash. Ashes and dust, baby. That's where you came from and that's where you'll end up."

"I'm getting tired of you," I say. I raise my head and a sparkle catches my gaze.

The ocean is just through the trees. And beyond that, something else. Something important.

Chapter 9

I stare out at the ocean and the building beside it. The concrete exterior is barely visible between palm trees and tall grass, which wisps in the wind. The metal roof gleams beneath the morning sun, and I blink away the glare.

A man strides toward the building. His white coat flaps against his jeans. He strides toward an opening in the side of the building then disappears inside it.
I lose my breath.
This time, it's not a side effect.

That's him. That's my salvation right there. All I have to do is make it to him.

"You'll never make it to him," Amy whispers. She giggles in my ear. I can almost feel her breath on my neck and the disdain in her stare.

"I'm losing it."

"It's cute that you thought you ever had it," she replies.

I ignore the grumbling of my conscience. She's got to be some weird manifestation of it. Unless, the disease is eating at my brain already.
I shudder the thought out and scramble to my hands and knees again. My heart rate increases.

I launch toward the gap between the trees. My feet slip in the dirt and I face plant.
The searing pain in my chin doesn't drown out the rat-tat-tat of gunfire over my head.

I roll onto my back and crane my neck.

40

The thugs are back. But these are different. They're not thug one and thug two in camo in black. They wear red shirts and khaki pants.
The man in front grimaces – it might be a smile. His lips twist around the scar which bisects his face.
I backpedal on my palms.

Scar face prattles off something in Spanish.
"No hable, uh, I don't speak Spanish." I shrug my shoulders. Maybe, these guys won't want to kill me.

"Dream on," Amy says.

"You work for the Escorpiones Negros?" the scar-free guy asks. He raises his gun and aims the cool steel at the center of my forehead. "You die, gringo."

"Please," I squeal. "I – look, this is all some big mistake. I got injected with a disease and if I don't find the scientist, then I'll –"

"Shut up," Scar-free says, jabbing the gun toward me.
I jam my mouth closed. My watch beeps on my arm and I lift it. I gaze at the long hand and inhale gasping breaths. Nearly an hour. An hour until I leave the world.

Wetness dribbles from my nostril and I don't bother touching it. It's another of the reactions. I've experienced everything from fire to ants to sweat that isn't there.

"Watch," Scarface says. He opens his palm to me.
I stare at it, wordless. What am I supposed to watch? There's nothing there.
"Oh shit, he's bleeding," Scar-free says and jabs his weapon forward again.

I touch my left hand to my nostril, and my fingers come away covered in blood. This time, it's for real.

"Watch," the guy says and crooks his finger.

They want my watch. A mid-jungle shakedown. This has to be one for the history books.
"I need it," I say, while clutching my wrist to my chest. "It tells me when I'm going to die."
"Gringo loco," Scar-free mutters. "We kill you now. Bam bam." His finger inches closer to the trigger.

"Wait." The scarred man pushes the gun's barrel aside and glares at his partner. He prattles in Spanish, anger in the hard lines of his face and the puckered, white scar.
His partner snaps at him.

I flip onto my front and scramble toward the trees. I'm a dog on all fours, evolving into a man. I'm up, running, fire burning in my lungs.
One of the men yells. The gunfire starts up again.

I dart behind a tree and bullets thwack into the other side of it.
"Shit," I grunt and barrel down the hill toward the warehouse. He's so close, and that means the cure is too.

My insides convulse and writhe inside my body, withered by the virus. Leaves slap across my face, and I raise my arm and slap the branch away.

Pop, pop, go the shots. Shouts ring between the trees. The distant glimmer of the metal roof beckons. I can't go on like this. My legs are wasted, my muscles a sloppy mess of lactic acid and disease.
"Oi," one of the men yells.

I circle a tree and press my back against it. The shouts continue. Heavy footfalls rush closer, crushing twigs and leaves underfoot.
I have to time this exactly right.

One, two, three…I stick out my foot and the thug runs into it. He trips, arms flailing, and he sails through the air and strikes a rocky outcropping, just in front of my hiding spot.
The sound is a wet crunch of breaking bone.
He slithers to ground and doesn't move.

"You've done it now," Amy whispers. "Look at you go. You've upgraded from selfish asshole to murderer."

"He's not dead." I heave in great gasps of air. Blood rushes in my ears. I can't hear a damn thing.

The thug lies on his side, the barrel of the gun poking out from underneath him. His back doesn't rise or fall, and a pool of blood gathers in the grass and muck.

"Told you," Amy replies. "You killed him."
I shake my head.
The other thug calls out close by.

"His friend is coming," Amy whispers. "Guess what he's going to do when he finds out about this? Guess."

"Shut up." I stumble forward on my lactic acid legs and grab the end of the gun.
I wrench it free from the man on the ground and it drags through the blood. I raise it and press it to my side.

The last time I worked a gun was on a ranch with my friend's rich uncle. I made a total fool of myself then. Now has to be different.
I check the safety on the side. It's clicked off.
I raise the weapon and take aim.

The thug strides around the tree, his rifle up. His gaze flickers to his compatriot on the ground, then back to me. Anger tightens the muscles in his jaw.
He yells wordlessly and squeezes the trigger.
Everything slows in time with the pained rhythm of my heartbeat.

I copy his movements and step to the left. The gun's barrel darts upward, and the butt punches me in the shoulder.
Rat-tat-tat-tat. Bullets spray upward. Two of them catch the thug. One in his chest.
His arm jerks back. The gun swings forward.

The second bullet slices through the meat of his cheek. He drops toward the jungle floor.

Time rushes back to its usual speed. I dive sideways, and the splatter of bullets tears up the ground and trunk behind me. I curl into a ball and grip the gun. My body hits the dirt and rolls to a halt.

Dust and silence rise.

I gag, and vomit splatters onto the grass in front of me. This time, it has nothing to do with the virus chewing through my insides.

"You killed two now. Well done." Amy's bitter whispers chase me to my feet.

Chapter 10

Palm trees sway in the ocean breeze, and that damn humidity from the jungle fades a little. I can finally breathe again, but those breaths, man, they rattle in my chest. Maybe the disease eats my lungs too.
Maybe I'm going to die before the two hours is up.

I raise my watch and stare at the ticking mechanism. A little over an hour left.

The warehouse shimmers into being in front of me. The concrete walls, the high windows, it's all so solid and real. This has to be the end of the line.
That scientist bastard is in there, and I'll shoot the shit out of him if he doesn't give me the cure.
I'm past caring.

I crouch low and move toward the opening on the side of the building. There's a car just ahead – one of those camo Jeeps – and it sets alarm bells ringing.
What if Mr. Scientist isn't alone?

I slip into the warehouse and halt behind a stack of wooden crates. Voices bounce off the high ceiling, thick with accents.
One British - my heart leaps, that's got to be him – and another Spanish.

The air in here is close, but the breeze from outside brushes the back of my sweat-streaked neck. The metal ceiling tings and crackles overhead, beneath the heat of the sun. It will be noon soon.
I'll die soon.

I edge forward an inch and peek between the wooden slats.

The scientist stands in front of a desk, crowded with tubes and syringes and all kinds of sciencey stuff I don't know or understand. His hands are up, and his expression is stricken with fear.
"You're too late." Amy's voice is a constant companion. It doesn't shock me anymore to have those poisonous words as an accompaniment.
The smooth, silver tip of a gun pokes the scientist in the forehead.

"This is it," Amy says.

"Please, you don't understand." The scientist's tone drips fear. "I'm doing the best I can."
"Then where is the money, scientist boy?" That thick, foreign accent sends shivers down my spine. I've heard enough of that to last me a lifetime.

I shuffle forward another inch, and the thug appears in my frame of view, dressed in a black shirt.
"Escorpiones Negros." Amy doesn't know any Spanish. The real Amy doesn't.
"I – the hotel explosion. I got distracted," the scientist whispers. "I'll find him. I'll get the money."
"Yeah, you will. You find the star, or I put bullets in your – " the thug says. A slow, wicked smile parts his lips and evil creeps onto his face. "No, I do worse than that. I kill your little girl, your little Lily, just like I killed your wife."

The scientist stumbles back. He drops to his knees and presses his palms to his eyes. "How do you know about her?"
"The boss, he know everything. Stupid Gringo." The thug lifts the butt of the rifle and poises it above the scientist's head.
I jerk forward and the crates rattle.

The thug halts, mid-swing, and stares in my direction.

"Wow, you're really good at this whole hiding and running thing, aren't you?" Amy asks. "Add it to the long list of shit you never do right."

I stay hunched and urge my legs to move. I rush toward another stack of crates, on the other side of the door.

"They're coming for you," Amy sings.

I skid to a halt behind the crates and hold my breath. My lungs burn from the disease or the lack of air. My vision fades in and out of blackness.

"You got friends in here, Gringo?" The thug marches to my old hiding spot and swings around the corner. He aims his gun at the position I've just escaped.

The scientist doesn't answer him. "Don't touch my daughter. She's not a part of this."
"She part of your family, so she part of this."
The black-clad thug's gaze travels to the open warehouse doors and sweeps across the crates and litter. He sniffs, then shrugs his shoulders. "Ratas," he mutters.

His boots scrape across the concrete floor and halt in front of the scientist.

"I'm doing everything I can."
"You do better or you die. Boss need the money today, or no more shipment for the mainland," the thug replies.

Drugs. That's what this is about. It's the only answer that makes sense. But how the hell did I get caught in this?
It can't be a case of bad luck. Can it?

The thug lifts his arm and stares at the cheap rip-off on his arm. "You got less than an hour. Make it happen or bam-bam, no more girlie. Got it?"
"Yes," the scientist whispers.

The thug thumps across the warehouse and out the door. A minute passes and a car engine starts up. Tires crunch outside, the hum intensifies then fades into the distance.

That noise is replaced by the hiccups and muted sobs from the figure in the center of the warehouse.

Chapter 11

I stalk out from behind the crates and keep low. Crying or not, this is the guy who injected me with the lethal disease in the first place. I pause in front of the warehouse doors and peer out into the bright, morning sunlight.

The coast is clear of Jeeps and black or red clad thugs. My heart palpitates, and I turn on my heel and stride toward the scientist, bravery bolstered by the gun at my side.
It clacks against my sweat-soaked shirt.

"You gonna kill him too?" Amy asks.

I halt in front of the man on his knees and lift my gun. I haven't even checked how much ammo I have left.
"You owe me an explanation."

The scientist jerks upright. His gaze travels from my worn loafers up to my slacks, past them to my shirt and face. "Oh my God," he says and whimpers.
He plants his palm on the 'crete and forces himself upright.

"Whoa, there," I say. "Don't make any sudden movements."
"Okay," he replies. "Look, I – I didn't want to do that to you. They made me do it."
"Who?" I ask, though the answer already brews in the back of my mind, simmering beneath the soupy surface of confusion, brought on by the disease this ass infected me with in the first place.
"Escorpiones Negros," the scientist says.
I stare at him for a second, then jerk the barrel of the gun upward. "Get up and explain."

He scrambles to his feet and doesn't bother dusting off his white coat, which is streaked with dirt. "The Black Scorpions," he replies and lifts his palms. "Look, I'll tell you anything you want to know, just don't shoot me."

I lower the gun and it clacks to my side. "It's not like I can." Big talk from the guy who tossed his cookies in the jungle after shooting the last two thugs. "Who are these Scorpion guys?"

"They're a Cuban drug cartel. Headed up by Frank Blanco. They're the reason you've been infected and I'm here," he says.

"They need money from you because they're running low on cash. Something about a shipment. I don't know all the details."

"They were the ones who blew up the hotel," I say, grimacing at the memory of the woman inside.

"No." He gives a slight shake of his head. He glances toward the door of the warehouse and balls his hands into fists. "That was the Red River Gang."

"Red River. Why does that sound so familiar?"

"It's been all over the news the past couple weeks. Relatively new cartel, taking over the Cuban islands. Massive exporter of cocaine. Exporter isn't the right word, but you get what I mean," he replies. His cheeks are still stained with those tears from earlier.

I ignore the guilt frothing across the shores of my conscience. The sooner I get the cure, the sooner I get off the island and away from this hellhole.

"They blew up the hotel?"
"Yeah, the Scorpions and the River are fighting over turf.
The hotel was just the start of it. This island's going to
transform into a war zone, if it hasn't already," the scientist
says, and finally his resolve crumbles. "I just want to get out
of here.
S-save my daughter."

"I don't understand how you even wound up here."

"Same way you did. I came by boat. Family holiday."

The clipped off sentences get to me. They crawl under my
skin. This guy is so spooked he can't even talk properly, and
I'm pushing him for more information.

"You're such a good person," Amy hums in my ear.

"They figured out where I was. They know everything."
The scientist strides to the desk and braces his palms on both
sides of his computer.
I don't even know his name.

"Who are you?"

That silence seeps between us.
Outside, the waves lap against the rocks and burst upward in
a roar of ocean spray.

"Edgar. I'm Edgar. And my daughter Lily is on this island."
He turns to me, desperation vibrating from every fiber of his
being. "I need to find her, but I'm stuck here until you pay
up."

"I don't have the money."I'm broke, man."

Edgar's eyelids flutter closed. "Please tell me this is a joke."
His British accent thickens.
"It's not a joke. I've just gone through a divorce.
My ex took me for everything. I – we didn't have a prenup.
Why am I telling you this? I don't have the money."
Edgar opens his eyes and studies me from head to toe. The
weight of the disease rests on my shoulders.

"I'm the only one who knows how to make the cure," he
says.
I don't like where this is headed.
He opens his mouth, then rams it shut again.

"What?"
I ask, because I already know what's coming. I just want to
hear him say it.

"They'll kill my daughter if they don't get the money. My
Lily."

"But I don't have the money."

"Yes," Edgar says and hangs his head. "And I don't have my
daughter. I'll cure you."

My heart soars to the ceiling and cruises at peak altitude.
Man, this could all be over soon. Granted, I still have to
escape from the island, without a phone or any help from –

"But you have to help me in return," he says and shatters my
naivety. "You have to find my daughter and get her to
safety." His gaze drops to the gun at my side.

"This?" I hoist it aloft. "I barely know how to use this."

"Agree to help me and I'll make the cure right now."

My watch beeps. Another ten minutes have slid by in a flash. "Fine," I say. "I'll help you find her."

Edgar presents his hand.
I stare at it like it's a trap.

"You, help?" Amy's disembodied voice circles my head, noise oscillating from left to right. "You're too selfish to help. You don't care about that little girl or this scientist, do you?"

I clench my jaw and grasp the scientist's hand. We shake on it, firmly.

At last, Amy falls quiet.

Chapter 12

The scientist releases my hand and turns back to his desk.
He grasps the mouse beside his laptop and clicks on a folder
on the desktop, right beside the blue Skype icon which is
ingrained into my brain.

I've taken so many conference calls on it, I have an allergic
reaction to the logo.

"Just a moment," Edgar says. "The file is encrypted."
A password box pops on the screen, and he types in his
password.
"I try to keep everything coded. I'm pretty sure they're
trying to hack my devices."

"That's comforting," I reply and grip the butt of the rifle. It's
a security blanket to me. Better than gripping the insides of
my pockets.

I blink and swallow bile. The warehouse pitches around me
and the ceiling quivers inward and outward, a great,
blackened lung, breathing around me.

"Sit down," Edgar says over his shoulder. "The more you
move, the faster the virus works on your internal systems."
That's comforting, given that I've spent the past hour
chasing after his ass.

I lower myself to the floor and brace my back against the
crates behind me. They teeter but don't topple over.
"What is all this stuff?" I ask.
"They're drugs or supplies," Edgar says and finishes typing
in the password.

The file opens and he examines a document on the screen. Simple words, below an equation.

Kind of like a recipe. "I haven't looked inside. They told me not to tamper with the crates or they'd murder my wife and kid."

"Your wife?"
He swallows air but doesn't reply.

"What is the formula, anyway?" I ask, but only because I've got nothing better to do.

"It's not too complicated. I just use the directions to make sure I have the right measurements of the stuff."

He snaps on a pair of latex gloves and works his fingers to the end.

"At least buy me dinner first," I say.

My watch beeps.
"We don't have time for niceties," Edgar replies. He then focuses on the screen. I'm officially dismissed.

I shut my eyes and listen to the wind outside instead. I hear the crash of waves on the rocks and the beach.
I imagine I'm lying out in the sun, in good health, a Mojito in my hand. Yeah, that's a good thought.

The wind whips outside. A thud-thud of noise lulls me into my happy place.
That thud-thud is the gentle beat of the ocean waves. It resolves into a sharper tuk-tuk noise, and my eyelids flicker open.
The warehouse jumps into sharp relief.

"What is that?" I ask.

The scientist freezes, syringe in hand, tubes of solution in front of him. His arm trembles, the clear fluid in the syringe washes against the glass inside. "Hide," he says. "They're coming, you must hide."
"But —"

"Now," he roars, spitting flies from his lips.
He drops the syringe next to the tubes and exits the formula sheet on the computer,
clicking frantically. "If they find out I'm helping you, they'll kill us both."

I scramble upright and vertigo shuttles me toward the ground again.
I strike out with my palms and graze them for the umpteenth time in an hour.

"Hurry up," Edgar growls. "Don't come out no matter what you see. No matter what happens. Understand?"
 I'm up again in a flash. I dart toward the crates at the far end of the warehouse and dive behind them.

The tuk-tuk of helicopter blades drown out all noise. They slow down at last, a whine of rotors. The bird is here, it's landed, and the scientist hurries across the room.
He shoves the syringe into an open drawer, then slams it shut.
He grasps the wooden surface and stares around wild-eyed.

The noise dies down further, shadows dance across the entrance to the warehouse.
Footsteps crunch closer and three men enter the warehouse, dressed in those black shirts and camo pants.
All three hold rifles to their sides.

Even if I happened to be a good shot, which I'm not, I wouldn't stand a damn chance.

They walk up to the scientist, and the one at the front, he's shorter and fatter than the other two, grasps Edgar's lab coat and drags him to the center of the room.

"What are you doing?" he shouts. His accent is clean compared to any other I've heard since I landed on this little slice of nightmare.

"N-nothing," Edgar replies, over the slowing whir of the blades outside.

"I – working for the boss."

"We know you accessed the folder," the main dude says.

Edgar's eyes widen. "I just wanted to make sure I'd be able to concoct it."

The fat man drags him closer and breathes into his face. Beady eyes rove up and down Edgar's body. "We're always watching. We always know."

"I swear to God, I didn't do anything I wasn't supposed to," Edgar replies.

The fat man spits in his face, then tosses him to the side. The two others catch him and laugh hysterically.

"You gonna cry, Gringo?"

"Cry like a little bitch," the other one says, and chuckles too.

"Where's my daughter?" he says, mocking Edgar's British accent.

" Where's my daughter?" The man continues to mock Edgar. He punctuates the end of his question with a slap. "Pig. You come with us now."

"But – the money. What if he comes for the money?" Edgar asks. "The Hollywood guy."

"It's too late for that now," the fat thug says. "Boss wants you at the compound.
Those scum Rivers have taken most of the island. No time for money. Only time for war."

The status changes so fast my head spins to catch up. Just how close was their base,
that they could fly over in the few minutes since Edgar accessed his cure folder. And how do they know?
The hack. It's because of that damn hack.

"You're coming with us," one of the other thugs says, dragging the scientist toward the door.

"No!" Edgar yells. "Lily!"

The men burst out laughing again. "Where's my daughter?"

Their mocking cries echo through the door and out into the sunlight.
My last sliver of hope for salvation disappears with them.

The helicopter's rotor whines again, the blades speed up and slice through the air.
 I rush out from my hiding place, toward the warehouse door.
I halt beside it and stare at the helicopter.

The black insect rose into the sky and tilted to one side. It soared toward the horizon.
I am alone.

Chapter 13

The helicopter settles on top of a building on the opposite shore. Minutes across the water, but too far for me to reach it in time.
What am I going to do? Storm a compound filled with thugs and dealers, weapons and drugs?

I grip the rough wall and dig my fingertips into it – a wakeup call. He's gone, and I need to figure this out by myself.
I turn and rush toward his laptop, my heart pounding against my rib cage.

"You're just going to let them take him away?" Amy's voice remains somber this time. It stabs my conscience and skewers me with guilt, but I keep moving.
Movement is life now. If I stagnate, the watch will continue beeping until the time runs out and I never again hear another alarm.

"Just like that? Seriously? He offered to save your life."
"He also injected me with a disease," I snap. Shit, now I'm talking to myself. "Edgar said I shouldn't come out, no matter what happens."

"I don't think that extends to his kidnapping," Amy says. "You have a gun. You're such a coward."

I force her words from my thoughts and scramble to the desk. The test tubes sit in front of the laptop, the fluid within rocking against the sides of the glass.
A gentle sway of motion chases the meniscus against the curve.
I move the steel holder aside and reach for the laptop instead. Everything is out. I just need the formula and the syringe Edgar hid in the desk behind me.

I check my watch and swipe my fingers across my brow. It comes away wet with sweat.

Forty-five minutes until I die.

I run my finger across the mousepad and click on the folder on the desktop. It's labeled FTC, but it's got to be the cure. It's the same one Edgar opened.
I click on the folder. A password box pops up on the screen.

Real panic clutches my heart in an iron fist and squeezes. I can't breathe, and I certainly don't know this damn password. I didn't think to ask.
I didn't think to look at the pattern of keystrokes beneath Edgar's pale, tapered fingers.

"Shit," I whisper.

"A coward and a fool," Amy whispers. "Now, that should be the title of your autobiography."

The fact that I've got a book out is a sore point for Amy and always will be. But this isn't Amy, this is her voice, a projection of my subconscious hate for myself.
And it doesn't matter.
"Come on," I whisper. I type a random combination of keys. Nothing happens. I'm screwed. "Please."

But I have no idea what the password is. There's got to be something here that'll let me in on his secret. I ram open a desk drawer and rifle through the papers, fingers streaking the pages with sweat. Nothing.
Useless formulas and chemical equations. Scribbled notes on the viability of testing one solution in comparison to another.
Gibberish.

The bloop-blip of a Skype call interrupts my frantic scrambling. I frown and straighten.

"What the hell?"

An unfamiliar name flashes on the screen, accompanied by the outline of a stock Skype profile picture. The blue and white man.
 "Black one?" I click on the green phone icon, more out of habit than anything else.
"Stay where you are," a man says. It's a normal call – no video.

"Who is this?" Hope flutters in my chest and replaces the panic for a couple seconds.
"You have our money, correct? The scientist, he says you have our money. If you pay up now, we bring him back and cure you."

My throat closes. Why would Edgar tell them that?

"Same reason you left him to die," Amy hisses. "He wants to live as much as you do. And he has more reason. He has a daughter."
"I – yeah, okay, I have the money," I say. "Bring him back."

"Liar." Amy laughs after whispering it.

"Good," the man replies, and his voice is gravelly and deeper than any I've heard before. "Good. You deposit the money into the account."

"I don't have the details," I reply. "Bring him back so I can get them."

"No, no. We send you the details on his computer. You're in front of it now."

I can't take much more of this. I can't take another forty minutes.

"Okay. Are you bringing him back?"
I have no money to give these bastards. Either they bring him back or I die.

"We bring him back after you make the deposit," the man says. "I —"
"You have five minutes to make the deposit. After that, we kill him." The line clicks off and an email bing through at the same time.

I don't bother opening it. I can't deposit money I don't have. So much for the gang not wanting money. Hadn't they said there was only time for war?

"He's going to die," Amy says, and for once, there's a tinge of sadness to her tone. "You've killed another one."

I turn and hurry toward the warehouse door. Wind pushes against me, and it's almost enough to drive me back a couple steps. My limbs are heavy as lead.
I grab hold of the gritty door jamb and stare out at the forest this time.

My eyes glaze over for a second, then spring back into focus with a snap.

"House," I mutter. "The house. There's got to be something there." The scientist lives in that rough building in the middle of the forest. Those boxes, the papers and files.

There has to be some evidence there, some record of his password.

It's the only hope I have left.

Chapter 14

"You're leaving? You know what this means for him, right?"

I don't answer Amy but focus on my destination; the line of trees which will lead me over the hill and toward that house. The wind, thankfully, blusters up behind me and forces me toward the jungle.

A narrow, pot-holed road stands between me and the destination. I hover behind a palm tree like a stalker and glance left and right.
Silence on the road. Not a car in sight.

I grab the rough bark of the palm tree and use it as leverage. I slingshot across the road, as fast as my jelly legs can carry me. They burn from the degradation of my muscles. Maybe they will soon turn into jelly.

I reach the line of trees and smash into one of them. I loop my arms around its trunk and shuffle until I'm in the forest. The warehouse roof glimmers beside the ocean. The doors are still open and empty, and waves rush the rocks and burst against them.
I've got to hurry. Hardly any time left now.

"I hope you die," Amy whispers.

"As opposed to all the encouragement you've given me up until this point," I say and turn on the spot. I stride up the hill, grabbing at low-hanging branches as I go. I tug myself along.
Step, tug, stumble, repeat. That's the only way I'm getting up this hill and to that house.
Gunshots snap in the distance, and I pinch my stolen weapon to my side. My shirt is soaked through with sweat and dirt.

I've transformed from Jay O'Connor to a refugee, trying to escape fate.

The bird calls and rustled leaves are now ominous, and the humidity closes in around me, brushing against my skin, demanding a price for my passage. And that price is more sweat and vertigo.

I sway and stop, eyes closed, palm flush against the rough bark of one of the trees.

"When we were younger, you used to come to bed with me," Amy whispers.

My eyes snap open. This time, I expect her to be in front of me. "What?"

"That's when it started. Before the engagement. Before your mother's death. You stopped caring about us."

"What the hell are you talking about?" I whisper. I don't have time for emotional blackmail, but the dizziness hasn't passed.

I push off from the tree and stalk up the side of the hill.

"You used to come to bed and hold me every night. We watched shows together or ate junk food, remember?" Amy's tone is soft, for once.

My foot connects with a root and I flop onto my stomach in the muck. I growl under my breath and leopard crawl forward, then rise onto all fours. "You're distracting me."

"You remember, though."

Of course, I remember. It'd been the best time of our relationship. Of my life, at least.

"And then, one night, you stayed up instead of coming to bed," Amy says. "I didn't think anything of it at first. But then it started happening every night. And I was alone."

What could I say to that?

I crawl forward and mud leaks through the knees of my slacks.

"At first I cried. Then I got angry. Then I gave up hope, and eventually, I realized it would never change," she whispers. "I checked out, emotionally. I cheated because it was an escape."

"And you call me a coward," I reply. "Why didn't you speak to me about it?"

"Because I knew you'd laugh it off or act like it was my fault. There was no point. So, I formulated my escape plan. And now, you're here, alone. Alone in the forest, dying, because all you ever cared about was yourself."

I grab and slither up a boulder. I plant my feet in the mud and stand straight. "This is bullshit. You're not really here."

"You're right. I haven't been with you for a long time," Amy replies, and a hint of laughter enters her voice now. "That's what happens when you abandon people. They turn their backs on you too. Such a simple mistake."

I don't know how to respond to any of this, so I settle for ignoring it.

"You can't ignore yourself."
I stumble on, between the tree trunks and over roots and grass, trampling mulch. Up, up, I go. Gunshots and muffled yells course through the jungle. The noises become quieter the higher I go, replaced by the oppression of heat and moisture.
I halt and rest my forehead against rough bark.

I waver, and a flash of gray catches my gaze. "There," I whisper.

The low-slung bunker appears between the trees, its black window empty as it was before, door ajar. The only difference is the tire tracks in front of it.

"Good luck," Amy says, and her voice fades. Hopefully, for good this time.

Chapter 15

I stumble through the door and bang against the concrete. The slam of steel reverberates through my brain and jars me to the core, but I don't stop.

My watch beeps again.

Another ten minutes. I'm like a balloon with a puncture. The air leaks out of my side and I deflate as time passes.

"Almost," I whisper.

The inside of the bunker greets me with dust and the gentle hum of quiet. My footsteps ring on the cement floor, and I focus on the opened cardboard boxes.
Edgar must have kept a copy of the password, somewhere. Right?

I hurry to the boxes and rip the top one open. I spare a glance for the trees outside, devoid of movement or life.
I am truly alone.

The cardboard brushes against my fingertips, and I rip out the journal on top. I flick open the leather cover and rifle through the pages. Snatches of Edgar's thoughts reach out to me from the past.

Lily is scared we'll –
Christmas day today. I bought Eliana a ring, but not sure she'll –

No, these entries are old. They're from before he came to the island. I toss the book aside and it thumps onto the floor.

I don't allow the pang of guilt to overwhelm me. These might be his thoughts, but my salvation might lie within their pages. I need to go through them as fast as possible.

I grab the next journal and lift it. My vision blurs and I blink three times. It clears again.
The pages are smooth under my fingertips, and dirt smudges across their corners. I bend my head and focus on the writing.
Sweat drips onto the page.

First day here, and I don't know what to do with myself.
Eliana isn't happy. Lily is terrified.
Bingo. This has to be from the start of his time on the island.
I turn and walk to the desk. There's a chair beside it, and I've got to sit down before I collapse.
I lower myself onto the hard surface and rest my back against the melamine rest.

I can't help feeling guilty about being here, but if we hadn't come, Eliana's brother would be dead. They still haven't given him to us.

I flip forward in the diary and halt on October 31st.
We can't stay in the hotel anymore. They're here, day and night. They stalk Eliana and threaten me when I come back from the warehouse. We've got to find somewhere else to live until this blow over.

I rifle through more pages.

November 22nd.
I found the place. It's a bunker out in the woods, close enough to the hotel for us to make an escape, tonight. They'll never find us there. Eliana wants to wait to find her brother, but it's too late for that.

I'm beginning to think they killed him a long time ago. We'll get to the bunker and hide. Then we'll organize a boat off the island before they can catch us.

Clearly, that didn't pan out. Empty pages fill the rest of November and most of the next month. If I didn't know better, I'd think they'd made their escape.

December 23rd.
I haven't been able to write because they've had me working day and night on something new. They found our bunker two hours after we disappeared, but not before we managed to hide Lily.
They've taken Eliana. They'll kill her if I don't do what they want.

Something new. That has to be the disease. I flick through the pages, and my pulse races to catch up. I creak back against the chair and swallow dry air. The inside of my mouth is dry as the desert.

December 31st.
I've done it. It's a disease. Truly horrific. They have to see I've done what they've asked. They have to let her go now.

And the journal ends there. I slap it shut and hang my head. There's got to be another one, more recent, but I don't have time to rifle through his thoughts. Not that I have a damn choice.

I need that password.

Noise scratches behind me, and I freeze. I choke on fear and swing the gun into position. My sweaty grip slips on the cold metal.
"What are you doing?" a voice asks, in a British accent.

I spin in the chair and raise the rifle, finger on the trigger.

A little girl, maybe about seven years old, stands in front of me, her white sneakers stained at the front. Her beige shorts have a rip in one side, and her shirt bears the likeness of SpongeBob SquarePants.

"Those aren't for you," she says, pointing at the journal in my hand.
Pieces of the puzzle click into place. I lower the gun and click on the safety for the first time since I stole it. "You're Lily."

Her eyes widen, and she takes a single step backward.
 "Don't be scared." I raise my grubby palms. "I'm a friend of your dad's. Edgar? He sent me to find you."

The kid has to know something about the passcode. Or maybe she doesn't, and I'm just the asshole giving her false hope.

"Where is he?" Lily asks. She takes another step back, around the cardboard boxes. She shields herself from view. Only her head peers out at me.

Lie or the truth? Lie or the truth?

"Some bad men took him away," I say. "But I can help you get him back."

"How?" Her gaze tracks down my body and up to my face. "You look like you're going to faint."

"That's the thing, kid. I'm real sick, and your dad was the only one who could make the cure.

But now he's gone and –"The crunch of tires on dirt slice through my words and my thoughts.

The journal drops from my grip and thumps to the floor.
I slip from the chair and drop into a crouch.

Every nerve ending in my body screams for me to stop moving.
Stop everything.
I'm going to die.

"They're here," Lily whispers. "Quickly. Come with me. I have a place to hide."

It's too much to hope.
I scrape across the floor and around the corner of the boxes.
Outside, footsteps stomp toward the entrance.

Lily hunches over and grasps a tiny ring in the floor. She lifts a grey lid with ease and points at a crawl space beneath the bunker. "My daddy made it," she whispers. "It's a fake floor."

I topple into the space and scoot to one side, against the far wall of the foundation. Lily follows me in. She shuts the trap door above our heads.

I'm plunged into darkness.

Hissing laughter whispers through the gloom, but it's not from Lily or anyone else. It's from inside my own mind.

Chapter 16

Pale, white light flares in the darkness and washes across my arms. All of my hairs stand on end, but the laughter disappears, at last.

Lily stands in the center of the space, her hand wrapped around a cord, which connects to a portable light.

"Don't worry," she whispers. "They won't be able to see this from up there."

The room beneath the bunker is at least as big as the space upstairs. A bed in the corner, a pot in the other for a toilet, and a shelf against one wall, stacked with books. Shit, there's even a mini kitchen, with a gas stove and a few cupboards.

"Mom used to come down and cook for me, but now I cook for myself," Lily whispers, gaze on mine.

She's older on the inside. She's seen too much for a kid her age, but I can't help that. I can't save her from all the bad things she's seen, nor can I wipe away my own memories.

Thumps ring out overhead. They've entered the bunker.
I didn't get a chance to see the colors of their shirts. Red or black, either way, they'll kill us both if they find us.
I press my finger to my lips to silence the girl.

The scent of excrement and dirt drifts on the air, mingled with stale food. How long could the girl survive here on her own? Not long enough.

Lily creeps closer, then sits down in front of me, legs folded. "I haven't seen anyone since my daddy left two days ago."

"I'm sorry," I say. Confusion rattles my brain. "I thought he came here today."
"No, but there was a lot of noise today." She breathes, low enough for me to hear and no one else. "Don't worry, if we talk this way, they can't hear us."

She's smart for a kid too.

"We came here a year ago. I was really scared, but mommy said we had to be here to help my uncle. Then bad stuff happened." She squeezes her eyes shut for a second.
They snap open again and she stares into my soul. "My mom is dead. My dad won't tell me, but I know she's dead."

"How?"

"She wouldn't leave me alone down here for this long without coming to visit," Lily replies.
I adjust my grip on the rifle and soothe myself with its weight.
This girl has been through more than I have, and that says a lot.
The thumping upstairs halts, just beside the trapdoor.
"Shit." I grimace at swearing in front of the kid. "Look, if that door opens, you close your eyes, all right?"

"Why?"

"Just do as I say."

A voice yells overhead. Gunshots are fired, but they don't penetrate the floor.

"What's happening?" Lily whimpers and presses her fists to her lips.

"They're fighting," I reply. I don't bother explaining the war. Or the men in different colored shirts. It wouldn't make a difference to her.

I stumble upright, and hunch over to keep from banging my head against the roof of the hiding place.
I stalk up to the trapdoor, hunch into a crouch, and aim the rifle at the flat square above our heads. I click off the safety on its side.

I'm the only hope we've got, bad shot or not.

Lily moves behind me and presses herself against the cupboard. She covers her ears and squeezes her eyes shut.

The room inhales. The calm before the storm.

Finally, the pop of gunfire halts, but I don't breathe yet. They're still up there. Someone won that fight, and the victor might be above my head.
The square of fake concrete rattles above our head, and dust bathes my face. I choke back a cough and blink the grit, eyes aflame.

The trap door lifts. Lily lets out a tiny squeal.

A man in a bright red shirt appears, gun aimed directly at my head.

I squeeze the trigger. The gun judders in my grip and bullets spray the space above us.

The thug reels backward, but he's not quick enough. Bullets slice through his vest, and one strikes under his chin. His head flicks back. Blood and brain splatters. He falls out of sight, except for his boots.

They dangle over the edge of the square gap to freedom, unmoving. A bit of gum sticks to the underside of the left one.

"Another one," Amy sings out.

I jolt and squeeze the trigger again. Lily screams behind me.

The bullets miss the guy's boot and crack into the ceiling of the bunker. More dust rains down. I drop the weapon and fall backward against the dirt. My head bounces and settles.

"Guy," Lily whispers. "Wait." Shuffling breaks out behind me, but I don't have the strength to turn my head and find her.

My gaze is glued to the hanging boot, the speck of gum. I drift away on a tide of blackness, and the last thing I hear is the beep of my watch.

Twenty minutes left to live.

Chapter 17

The aquarium in my agent's office bubbles behind him. He's got one of those machines that sends pockets of air to the surface. It always reminds me of one of my favorite kid's movies, but I never tell him that.

Roger is far too serious.

Today, he's dipped past serious and into the realm of morose.

"What is this?" He rasps and slaps down the notice on the walnut desk.

I don't bother leaning in to read it. I know what it says, because my publicist emailed it to me before she sent it to him.

"It is what it is," I say - a habit I picked up running with the top dogs. "Look, it's a business decision. Strictly professional. No harm, no foul."

"You don't know the meaning of professional, O'Connor." Roger sighs.

It's not the reaction I expect. "Uh, you do realize I just fired you, right?"

Roger rises from the desk and walks to the aquarium. He lifts a jar of fish food from the counter beneath it, pops off the lid, and reaches inside. He draws out a pinch full of flakes. "Whose idea was this?"

"It was mine," I reply. The lie sits like a fist in my chest.

"You're getting big now, Jay. You're starring in movies, instead of soaps. You made a lot off *Apocalypse Now or Never*."

My worst film. Cheesy as hell, but at least I made money off it.

"But if there's one thing I've learned in Hollywood, it's that you're never too big to hit the bottom again," Roger says, sprinkling flakes across the surface of the water.
The fish inside swim to the surface and open their vacuous mouths. They gulp down the food, greedy for more.

"And how you treat the little people on the way up, dictates how hard you fall when you do."

Roger places the can beside the tank again. He turns back to me, his eyes ablaze. It's not hatred in his gaze, but pity. "And trust me when I say that you will fall. You've just got to hope you're strong enough to survive the drop."

"I'm not falling and I – okay, fine, it was Tammy's idea. We just don't see a need for you anymore." Guilt trips across my mind.

"A need – well." He actually gives a little chuckle. "Who am I to argue with the publicist?

Look, kid, you've got to do what's right for you, I get it. But this isn't the way you go about it. You should've spoken to me first."

He lifts the notice from his desk, crumples it into a ball, then takes aim and bops it into his mesh wastepaper basket. "You owe me that much."

"Owe you?" I slam out of my seat and stand, fists clenched. "I don't owe anyone."

Roger shakes his head and pinches the bridge of his nose. "You've got a lot to learn. You won't get far with that attitude."

I glare at him, and my eyes burn a hole in the top of his bald head. How dare he speak to me like this? Who does he think he is?

"I don't need you," I growl. "I don't need anyone."

I storm out of his office, my polished shoes crushing his pale, yellow carpet.
"You're going to need help one day, kid. You'd better hope you've got friends left by then."

Roger's voice haunts me down the hall and into… Darkness.

Sobs echo through the black surrounds and shuttle me toward a pinprick of light. Muffled pleas reach me and tug me onward, upward.

"Please, guy, please. I need help. My daddy –"

That voice is familiar. A squeaky, fearful thing, smaller than I feel right now.

I hasten toward the pinprick of light, raise my arms, and snap to myself.
My eyes stare at the gap in the ceiling. A pair of black boots hangs over the lip of concrete.

The watch beeps on my arm.

"Shit," I grunt.

"Mister!" A girl bobbles into view, her cheeks streaked with tears. It's the scientist's daughter, Lily. She grasps my arm and waggles it. "You're awake."

"Yeah." I lift my arm, and it's like swimming through mud. I squint at the dial. "Ten minutes."

"What's the matter?" she asks. A tear hangs on the bottom lashes of her eyelid. It dangles there, caught in a state of perpetual anticipation. Will it fall? Will it stay there and evaporate?

"I need to find the cure to my disease," I say through gritted teeth. "Your dad was making it for me, before they took him away. There's a recipe for the stuff on his computer, but it's locked behind a password."

"I know the password," Lily whispers.
I grapple with the gun beside me and sit upright. "You know it?"

"Yes, he told me in case something bad happened. A long time ago. I still remember it." Lily looks up at the dead man above us and pulls a face.

"I have to get that cure. Will you help me?"

Lily hesitates. She looks from the boots of the dead thug to my face. "Yes. Will you help me find my daddy?"

I swallow, and my throat constricts, then loosens again. "I'll try my best." It's the best I can offer at this point.

We probably won't be able to make it back to the warehouse and concoct the cure in time for my survival. But it's the only hope I've got.

"You always were a determined son of a bitch," Amy says.

I jump at the sound of her voice in my right ear.

Lily gasps and claps her hand over her mouth. "Are you okay?"

"Fine," I say. As fine as I can be. "Let's get to the warehouse. It's close." Not close enough for us to walk.

And I definitely can't run.

"Can you help me up?" I ask.

Lily's tiny, pale face fills with determination. "Yes." She slips her small hand beneath my elbow and heaves.

Chapter 18

The blood of the man I shot pools around the cardboard boxes and embraces the scientist's journal. The side of the book is stained red, and the writing is probably illegible. I stare at it and shuffle toward the front door.

Lily grasps the underside of my forearm, and I grip the gun in turn.

"We're almost there," Lily says. "Almost at the door."
"I can't walk all the way there." I lean a little too heavily on the girl. She's tiny. She won't be able to drag me there, and my muscles are finally starting to give up. I'm almost a rag doll.

"Die, you selfish bastard." Amy's voice deepens to a growl.

Lily guides me out of the doorway and into the jungle. The dead man's car sits in front of the bunker, its wheels in the hollowed-out tire tracks and the key in the ignition.
"Thank God," I mutter.

"I can't drive," Lily says.

I haven't laughed in what feels like years, but a chuckle burbles from my lips. She can't drive. "Don't worry. I'll drive," I say. "Just get me around to that side of the car."

The car is nameless and topless, decorated in beige and pale green camouflage, with black rungs forming a cage across its top.

Lily and I stumble up to the driver's side. She grasps the handle and jerks the door open, then helps me inside. I strain onto the high step, every nerve screaming for release.

Would it really be so bad to die? Anything is better than this abject torture.

I swing my feet toward the pedals, and they drag across the rubber mat on the floor. The gun pokes into my side and I wince.
Lily slams the door shut. She rushes around to the other side and hops in.

"Are you buckled?" she asks.

I shake my head and don't bother reaching for the belt. I'm not wasting time on that. I turn the key in the ignition and the engine roars to life. The thunderous hum of gas guzzling through the pipes sends me to Nirvana.
I am so close I can taste it.

The tire tracks in the road lead down the hill. I can judge the direction to the warehouse. Everything blurs around me, and I cling to the wheel, desperate to see again.

Lily gasps beside me.

Movement in the trees to the right. I swing my gun up and take aim. The girl dodges out of the way. My vision clears. Another thug, also in a red shirt, paces toward me, weapon raised.

"Oi," he shouts, then utters something in Spanish.

I squeeze the trigger and prepare for the judder of the gun, but it doesn't come.
The gun clicks instead. The magazine is empty.

"Shit." I toss the gun out of the car and press my foot flat on the gas. The car lurches forward and bullets spray from the end of the thug's gun. They pepper the side of the vehicle and the ping of metal stings my ears.

"Shit." That's what my vocabulary is reduced to. The watch will beep soon.

"Time is the one thing you need, and the one thing you don't have," Amy whispers.

Lily sits up beside me, her hands clamped over her ears and terror dominating her gaze.
The car rocks over roots and bumps in the dirt road. She wobbles in her seat but doesn't scream or cry.

I focus on the road again and steer away from a tree, my eyeballs rattling in my sockets like dice in a cup.

The gunfire fades, but the lack of noise doesn't bring me any comfort. We rocket down the hill toward the pitted road. Flashes of water appear between the trees.

"Almost there." I rattle the words out between gritted teeth. Agony courses over my skin and rips at my internal organs.
"Almost dead," Amy hums.

We burst through the trees and I swing the wheel right. The warehouse is close by, the roof glints in the distance.

"There," I say, pointing over the wheel. My index finger quivers. "That's where we'll find your father's laptop."

The girl doesn't say a word, but clings to the edges of her seat. She stares at our destination, unflinching. She'll do what it takes.
I accelerate toward the warehouse, mount the grass, and screech to a halt beside the open doors.

Chapter 19

Lily loops her arm through mine and drags me toward the door. I stumble and raise the other one. The sun bakes the back of my neck, moisture slides down my spine and pools above the lip of my slacks.
The warehouse swims toward me through the haze.

"Few more steps," Lily says, but her words sway in and out of my consciousness.

A few minutes left to live.

Will there be enough time to cook up the damn cure?

We enter the warehouse and the cool rush of air grants me a little energy. I straighten from my hunch and smack my lips to wet them. That doesn't work for shit.
"He put the syringe in the desk drawer." I point to the wooden table opposite the counter which holds the laptop.

Lily lets go of me and I stumble into a stack of crates. They're solid as bricks. I brake against them and drop to the warehouse floor.
The girl stops beside me and touches my shoulder, but I shake her off.

"Go," I say, while pointing to the desk. "I'll be fine."

She rushes toward the drawer, her steps light.
I scan the room for danger but find the laptop instead. It's there, exactly where I left it after that creepy Skype call. The screen is black, though the power button's light glimmers in the half-light.

Two Hours to Live

Windows line the upper half of the warehouse and a few beams of light enter and illuminate a square of floor just behind Lily.
I grasp the crate beside me and use it to pull myself upright. I grunt and drag myself toward the seat in front of the laptop, and the steel holder which contains the tubes we need to create the cure.

I step away from the crates and toddle across the space. I then collapse onto the chair, forearms grasping the cushion. Lily yelps at the noise but doesn't halt her search.

I force myself upward again and half-slide, half-crawl into the chair.

Amy's voice has gone silent. Her snarky comments have dissipated now that I'm close to death. It's probably because my brain is dissolving into a neural mulch in my skull. I'll probably start leaking out my ears.

I don't have the energy to shudder.

Lily jogs to my side, syringe in hand. "I found it." She raises the thing, triumph in her gaze.

"The password," I say, nodding toward Edgar's laptop. "Hurry." My fate rests in the hands of a child.

Lily hurries to the laptop and presses the spacebar. The welcome screen flares, and she clicks on a small icon in the center of the screen. "Which one?" she asks.

"The folder on the desktop. It's labeled FTC."

She clicks on it, and the passcode box pops up with an 'error' bong noise.

Her small fingers flutter across the keys and type out a password.
Curiosity nudges me. "What is it?"

"ElianaLilyLove." Her voice catches in her mouth. She's muffled by the emotion in her tiny frame, but she doesn't cry. Brave kid.

The folder opens and she clicks on the document within. It opens, and I can hardly believe it. This can't be happening.

"Pity," Amy whispers. My brain hasn't mushed into non-existence after all. "I thought you'd die for sure."

"Bad luck for you," I mutter, and my eyelids drift closed.

"Are you all right?" Lily asks.

"Fine," I reply, but I don't open my eyes. "The stuff is there. I think it's labeled."

Amy's laughter circles my head again. Left ear, right ear, left again. "I should've known you'd make it through this. You're a cockroach. You can't kill a cockroach."

"Better a live cockroach than a dead one," I growl.

"Mister?" Lily taps my arm.

I open my eyes and stare at her, but her face doesn't resolve into features. It remains a pale blob in the center of my line of sight.

"What's your name?" she asks. Something glimmers in her hand. Is it the cure?

"Don't you watch movies, kid?" I shake my head. "Didn't see Apocalypse Now or Never?"

"No," she replies. "My daddy says movies are junk and that I should read more books."
"Much good it did him," I mutter.

"Asshole," Amy says.

I clear my throat and blink again. The images in front of my eyes still don't resolve. "Jay O'Connor's my name. And don't you forget it."
Lily doesn't reply.

"I think I'm going blind. Do you have the cure, kid?"

"Not yet." She backs away. Glass clinks at the desk and her misty shape rushes to and fro, from the light of the laptop to the bench.

My body slumps. I slip sideways and tumble to the concrete. My skull bounces on the floor.

"Mr. O'Connor," Lily shrieks.

"I'm fine," I say, around a too-thick tongue. "Bine. Binnish the ure."
"You sound like a cartoon. Look at you. Your last moments are undignified. Nothing left of you but a shell," Amy says, and I hear her footsteps this time.
Or – wait, what is that? A helicopter?

"Someone's coming," Lily says.

I open my mouth to speak but nothing comes out, and my throat burns.

Lily's shape rushes toward me on the floor. "I have it, Mr. O'Connor. I have the cure. I think."

"In neck." I manage to speak.

She punctures my neck without hesitation and depresses the syringe's plunger. Like father, like daughter.

I wait for sweet relief, but all I get is the steady tuk-tuk of helicopter blades slicing the air.
"Did it work?" Lily whispers. "We have to run. They're coming. We have to find my daddy. He'll know what to do."

Her daddy is too far out of reach and I'm weaker than I've ever been.
My eyes drift closed, and darkness embraces me. It's so cool. It rocks me in its arms.

"Mr. O'Connor," Lily whispers. I shake from head to toe – no, she shakes me. "Please. I need your help."

I drift away on a wave of sleep.

Chapter 20

Jill stands beside the open office door and grasps a handful of yellow messages. She glances down at them, then meets my gaze. "Mr. O'Connor."

"Jill." I type another sentence of the script I've worked on for the past two months. Apocalypse Now or Never 2. It won't come together, no matter how much I write or how many collaborators I bring in.

"I've got your messages," she says, and her voice quavers.

She's only been working with me for a week, and she still hasn't dropped the whole, Mr. O'Connor thing, no matter how much I ask.

"Messages." I backspace a line of script. "I'm kind of in the middle of something here, Jill."

"I know, sir, but this one is important. It's from your wife," Jill says, and that timid tone strengthens into something akin to determination.

It's got to be serious if Jill won't sidle back into obscurity at the flick of my hand.

I raise my gaze from the screen and past the leather chair in front of my rosewood desk. My home peers at me from the exit to the room, along with a set of marble stairs beyond. One of the perks of fabulous wealth and fame – working from home.

"What is it?" I ask. "What does she want this time?"

"She called from the hospital," Jill says, and her grip on the papers goes white knuckled. "It's your mother, Mr. O'Connor. She passed away an half hour ago."

I stare at my assistant, expression blank. Inside, numbness washes over my brain and into my soul.

My mother is dead.

She's finally gone. All those weighty years of disappointment and lack of pride should lift from my shoulders. If anything, they settle deeper.
She's gone.
"Where's Amy?"

"She's with the – uh, body," Jill whispers, and her fingers flutter to her rose-pink lips. "I'm so sorry, Mr. O'Connor."
"Call me Jay." I turn my gaze back to the screen and type another line of text.

"Do you want me to get your wife on the line?" Jill asks.

I snatch a pair of glasses off my face – more for show than utility – and glare at her. "What? Why?"

"I – oh." Jill's jaw drops. She nods once and backs out of my office. The door swings behind her and shuts with a gentle click.

"Thank God that's over." I focus on the script once more.

A bright pinprick of light sits in the center of the page. I blink and lean in closer. It swirls toward me, and I duck my head.

Blackness and then…

"He's alive," a man yells, somewhere above me.

My eyelids flutter open and sound rushes in to greet me. Several men gather around my body, and none of them wear camo.
Instead, they're dressed in red overalls, printed with the words 'Coast Guard' on the breast. I'm safe.

"Can you walk?" one of the men asks.

I raise my arm and he grabs it. They haul me upright. My legs actually move; they work. I can see again.
The cure. It worked. I'm alive. It's over!

"We need to get out of here," I immediately say. My limbs are still weak from the beating they've taken. I don't want to know what my insides look like. "I need to get to a hospital, as soon as possible."
"Right this way," the coast guard says, and his warm smile fills me with the kind of joy I felt on Christmas morning as a kid.

"No," a voice yelps behind me.

Everyone freezes. I turn my head, ever so slowly, and catch Lily's face in my peripheral. Shit, I forgot about her.

"You promised," she whispers. "My daddy is on one of the islands out there. We have to go find him. You promised."

I stare at her. Shit, everyone stares at her. The guy beside her bends and places a blanket around her shoulders. "It's okay," he says. "You're safe now."
"We're safe." I repeat his words.
 Amy's voice doesn't come to me now. The haze of madness has lifted, like a bad dream I wish I couldn't remember.

I know what she'd say now. I refuse to think about it.

"My dad isn't safe," Lily replies, and she shrugs off the blanket. "You promised we would find him." Her chin wobbles and tears spill onto her cheeks. "My daddy." Gunfire pops outside the warehouse, not too far away.

"We must go, now," the coast guardsman says. He tugs me toward the exit. "This island is a war-zone. If we stay here, we'll die."
Lily wails behind me. She screams and sobs. I glance back. One of the other men lifts her from the ground and carries her out of the warehouse. She kicks and screams, balls up her fists, and strikes his back. He doesn't put her down.
"Stop it," the man says.
 She doesn't listen.

Her screams chase me out of the warehouse and toward the helicopter. The blades slice the air over and over again. The pilot adjusts his helmet behind the screen, and beckons for us to hurry the hell up.

They pile me through the side door and into one of the seats. Lily is forced in beside me. She tries to dart out of the door, but the coast guardsman holds her down.
 The doors slide shut. Safety at last.

The helicopter blades whine, and we launch off the ground and toward the sky. The island fades into the distance, replaced by the cool, blue of the ocean.
 "My daddy," Lily whimpers.
I turn my head away and look out the other window.

Epilogue

Eleven years have passed since the island.

The man, Jay O'Connor, sits at his desk and scribbles his signature along the bottom of another contract.
I saw his remake of what happened on the island.
He transformed my pain into a blockbuster for the world to enjoy.

I watch him from upstairs, my leather-gloved hand gripping the hilt of a katana. He hasn't seen me yet, and he won't until I'm ready for that to happen.

Every minute of every day has led up to this. From the moment I was delivered into the hands of my aunt and uncle, fresh off the Coast Guard's helicopter, to present day, this very moment.

I move onto his marble stairs and descend. My heels click with each step.

"Huh?" Jay spins in his leather judge's chair. He lays eyes on me. Confusion, followed by intrigue, then arousal quashed by fear.

Countless pitiful emotions. The same kind I felt years before. "Hello, Jay. Do you remember me?"

I can't help toying with him before the end.

The frown lines on his forehead deepen. He's attractive, even though gray dusts his temples now and streaks through his thick brown hair.
I remember that hair, slick with sweat. I catch a whiff of an ocean breeze, salt on the air, but it's all in my mind.

"Who – how did you get in here?"

"You left my father to die eleven years ago today."

The wrinkles smooth immediately, and clarity enters his gaze. "It can't be."

I raise the sword from my side and swing it up to shoulder height, parallel to the floor.

He stares at the blade. "Lily."

THE END

Two Hours to Live

Experience the Interactive Version

The story doesn't have to end on the page.

Two Hours to Live is also available as an interactive story app, where you can experience Jay's race against time in a different way.

Read the story with an adaptive musical score, guess the plot to help keep Jay on track, answer comprehension questions to win back time, and solve word scramble and word search puzzles as the clock keeps ticking.

Read the thriller. Hear the tension. Play to keep Jay alive. Look for **Two Hours to Live** interactive version at https://nevesterburton.com.

Listen to the Audio Version

The countdown does not stop when you close the book. Experience *Two Hours To Live* as an audiobook and hear Jay O'Connor's fight for survival unfold with pulse-pounding intensity.
Every threat, every chase, and every desperate second is brought to life through a cinematic narration that pulls you deeper into the island and the danger waiting there.

Perfect for fans who want to experience the story on the go, the audiobook delivers the thriller in a bold new format.

Audiobook edition available through most major audiobook platforms. Availability may vary by retailer and region.